SIMON & SCHUSTER BOOKS FOR YOUNG READERS
An imprint of Simon & Schuster Children's Publishing Division
1230 Avenue of the Americas
New York, New York 10020

Originally published in Great Britain in 1996 by Andersen Press, Ltd.
First American Edition, 1997.

The text of this book is set in 15-point Novarese Book
The illustrations are rendered in water color

10 9 8 7 6 5 4 3 2
Library of Congress Cataloging-in-Publication Data
Grindley, Sally.
Why is the sky blue? / written by Sally Grindley ; illustrated by Susan Varley.
p. cm.
Summary: Although he wants to learn all that wise old Donkey knows,
Rabbit cannot sit still to listen to the answers to his questions,
but in the end he teaches Donkey some new things.
ISBN 0-689-81486-0
[1. Donkeys—Fiction. 2. Rabbits—Fiction.] I. Varley, Susan, ill.
I. Title.
PZ7.G88446Wh 1997
[E]—dc20 96-35362

Why Is the Sky Blue?

BY SALLY GRINDLEY ILLUSTRATED BY SUSAN VARLEY

SIMON & SCHUSTER BOOKS FOR YOUNG READERS

RABBIT AND DONKEY lived in the same field.

Donkey spent his days in the corner nodding his head wisely and chewing on grass.

Rabbit popped up all over the place. His burrow had many openings, and he used them all.

Donkey was very old and knew a lot of things.

"I am very old," he told anyone who would listen, "and I know a lot of things."

Rabbit was very young and wanted to learn.

"I want to learn everything there is to learn," said Rabbit.

"I will teach you what I know," said Donkey, "which is a lot. Listen and you will learn."

"Goody," said Rabbit. "Yes, please."

And he jumped and he ran and he rolled and he bounced across the field and back again.

"I will teach you what I know," said Donkey, "which is a lot. But I will only teach you if you sit still."

"I will sit still," said Rabbit. "I will sit still and listen."

Donkey began. “I am going to tell you why the sky is blue.”

“Goody,” said Rabbit. “I really want to know why the sky is blue.”

But before Donkey had gotten very far, Rabbit wanted to know why the earth is brown. And before he had gotten any further, Rabbit was jumping around the field pointing at yellow flowers and red berries and white butterflies.

Donkey chewed on a piece of grass and waited. When at last he came back, Rabbit said eagerly, "I found out why berries are red. Shall I tell you why?"

"I know already," said Donkey. "And today's lesson is over now."

"Oh, but I missed why the sky is blue," said Rabbit. "And I really want to know why. Can I come back tomorrow and have another lesson?"

"I will only teach you if you sit still and listen," said Donkey.

"I will sit still," said Rabbit. "I will sit still and listen."

"Then tomorrow I will teach you what I know," said Donkey, "which is a lot."

Rabbit leapt in the air in excitement and ran and rolled and bounced across the field all the way home to dinner.

The next day, Donkey began again to tell Rabbit why the sky is blue. But before Donkey had gotten very far, Rabbit wanted to know about the sun and the moon and the stars. And before he had gotten any further, Rabbit was rushing around pointing at the clouds and the shapes of giant foxes and owls he could see among them.

Donkey chewed on a piece of grass and waited.

When at last he came back, Rabbit said eagerly, "Sometimes you can see the moon even when the sun is out."

"I know that," said Donkey. "And today's lesson is over now."

"Oh, but I missed why the sky is blue, again," said Rabbit. "And I really want to know why. Can I come back tomorrow and have another lesson?"

"One last time," said Donkey. "But I will only teach you if you sit still and listen."

"I will sit still," said Rabbit. "I will sit still and listen."

"Then I will teach you what I know," said Donkey, "which is a lot."

Rabbit leapt in the air in excitement . . .

. . . and ran . . .

. . . and rolled . . .

. . . and bounced . . .

. . . across the field all the way home to dinner.

The next day, Donkey began again to tell Rabbit why the sky is blue, but before he had gotten very far, Rabbit wanted to know why birds could fly and he couldn't. And before he had gotten any further, Rabbit was running up a slope and leaping off it making bird noises and flapping his paws.

Donkey chewed on a piece of grass and waited.

Rabbit didn't come back.

Donkey chewed some more and then looked across the field. He couldn't see Rabbit anywhere. He began to worry.

"He's young," he said to himself. "He might have gotten into trouble. I'd better go and find him."

He set off slowly across the field. After a few steps he came to a clump of yellow flowers. He looked among them for Rabbit. Rabbit wasn't there, but he watched the bees collecting pollen from the flower heads.

"It sticks to their legs," he said to himself. "I never noticed that before."

He set off again, more quickly this time, and as he trotted along he looked at the sky and saw woolly sheep among the clouds.

"It's a long time since I played that game," he thought to himself.

He came to the top of the slope that Rabbit had run down. He looked around to make sure no one was watching, then he began to gallop. When he reached the bottom he galloped on, enjoying the wind tugging at his ears and ruffling his coat.

"It's been a long time since I felt that feeling," he thought to himself.

And then he saw Rabbit, sitting quite still in the middle of a bush.

"Shhh," said Rabbit when he saw Donkey.

"I was worried about you," said Donkey. "What are you doing?"

"I'm counting the spots on ladybugs," said Rabbit. "Did you know that some have more spots than others?"

"No," said Donkey, "I didn't know that. I know a lot of things but I didn't know that. Let me see."

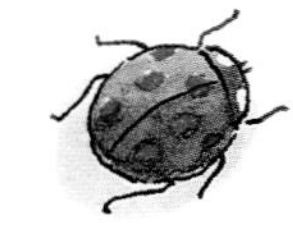

Rabbit and Donkey looked together. They sat still and counted spots until Rabbit began to yawn.

"Donkey," said Rabbit, "can you lift me out of here? I'm stuck."

Donkey smiled. "Hang on to my ears then," he said, lowering his head so that Rabbit could reach. He pulled him out and set him on the ground.

"Come," said Donkey, "I'll take you back home. Today you've taught me something new. Tomorrow I will teach you why the sky is blue."

"But I know why the sky is blue," said Rabbit.

"You do?" said Donkey.

"It's because that was the only color left in the paint box," said Rabbit.

Donkey smiled. Donkey laughed. Donkey cheered and kicked his legs in the air. Then he jumped and he ran and he rolled and he bounced, across the field and back again.

"That's the funniest thing I've heard in a long time," said Donkey. "Climb on my back and I'll carry you, but you must sit still."

"Donkey," said Rabbit. "Why *is* the sky blue?"

"Wait until morning," said Donkey.